# Minecraft: Isle of Adventure

## A Minecraft Novel

# Prologue: At the Bottom of a Hole

The shambling creature, body clothed in rags and tatters, stumbled toward me, arms outstretched. Cold hands closed around my throat as I stared into the thing's dead eyes. I should have been panicking. I should have been planning a daring escape. But all I could think, as it choked the life from me, was, "This is all Cook's fault."

# Chapter 1: The Best

Cook was our cook, in case that wasn't obvious. It occurs to me now that she probably had some other name that she used at home, or when around other cooks, to keep things from being confusing. But Mother always called her Cook, and Father never addressed her at all, and so Cook is what I called her, too.

She was the best cook in the country, obviously, because Father employed her. Everything Father had was the best. His hunting dog, Shropshire Shandyapple IV, was the best hunting dog for miles around. The best at tracking a fallen duck-chicken, the best at bringing down a rampaging wild cow, the best at accidentally mauling some dirty farmer's flock of sheep, and the best at growling menacingly while Father punished the dirty farmer for trying to poison his prize hunting dog with filthy, sick-looking sheep.

And, of course, Father had the best son. I'm not bragging, you understand. I'm simply a product of my upbringing. Father picked the best wife to have me, the best nannies to raise me, and the best tutors to teach me everything I know (and if I ever acted up, like the time I insisted to Professor Gandyhorn that he was wrong about the distance from the moon to the earth (implying that the Professor was NOT the best tutor money could buy, and thus disrespecting Father), he employed the best punishers in the land to correct my ways). I still remember the look of pride in Father's eyes when I showed him the red marks on my arm from where Master Freym had corrected my tendency to fidget. "Quality work, that," he had grumbled in his deep Father voice. I positively swelled with secondhand praise.

Which leads us to the subject of Cook, who, despite being the Best Cook in the Country, was quite dire in the kitchen. Her hire had been one of Mother's conditions for marrying, as she had grown up with the old peasant woman and refused to leave her behind. Father had grumbled, in his grumbly Father way, and agreed. A few years later, he held a grand cooking competition, forced Cook (a quiet old woman whose only passion in life seemed to be potatoes) to enter, and then declared her the winner. Father always had the best.

Which led, indirectly, to my being throttled to death by a walking corpse on a wind-swept island in the middle of the ocean. Because Cook hadn't put enough sugar on my stewed apples.

This was on the ship, of course, a few days before my encounter with the unfortunate dead gentleman with the surprisingly strong hands. Father had decided it was time for my formal schooling to begin, or at least that it was time for Professor Gandyhorn to stop living in our mansion, eating our food, and stealing our silver. And so, he asked Uncle (His Majesty King Stephen the Third, May He Rule in Peace) where I should be sent, and Uncle (His Majesty King Stephen the Third, May He Rule in Peace) said he had heard some good things about the Longshire Academy over the sea in Umbria, and why not send me there? I've always suspected that Uncle (His Majesty King Stephen the Third, May He Rule in Peace) has never entirely forgiven me for the time I dumped a bottle of syrup on Cousin Brandy (Princess of the Realm, Hope of the Nation)'s empty little head.

And so my bags were packed, and Mother cried, and I cried, and even Father sounded slightly hoarse as he yelled at the servants, and I was lead to the dock where The Spotted Narwhale waited to sail me to Umbria, with Cook to keep me company and fed.

All was well, until the third night of our journey, when my dinner consisted of roasted duck-chicken, lightly grilled salmon, a salad of tossed greens, broiled potatoes (Cook had been asked not to bring any of the vile spuds on the journey, but I relented when the old woman burst into tears) and, tragically, stewed apples. With the first bite of these, I knew something had gone horribly wrong. Had Cook taken leave of her senses? Was she trying to poison me? The apples didn't have enough sugar! Each bite made me angrier and angrier, the apple's natural sweetness like acid in my mouth. Finally, I had had enough. I hurled the bowl aside, stomped to the cabin door, hauled it open, and was immediately swept overboard by the titanic storm the ship had apparently been sailing through while I ate.

# Chapter 2: Waterlogged, but Witty

I awoke with water in my boots, sand in my mouth, and the sun beating down on my handsome pale skin. Spluttering and spitting, I dragged myself upright despite the weight of my (expensive, ruined, and) waterlogged clothes, and looked around at my surroundings. A quick checklist may please the reader.

Sand: Quite a bit of it.

Trees, on the far side of the sand: Present and accounted for.

Water, in vast quantities, stretching to the far horizon: Yes, indeed.

Food, visible and easily procured: Little to none.

Rescue ships, full of sailors, soldiers, and minor functionaries, deeply concerned with my well-being: None at all.

"I am on a deserted island. It's like a book," I said to myself, and then spat, because there was still sand in my throat. The adventure novels Father had permitted me to read had mostly been about dragons and mermaids and heroics. They hadn't covered what to do when you have sand in your teeth and the nearest toothbrush is a hundred miles away and sailing further by the second.

At this point, I saw no reason to panic. Surely, someone would soon notice that I was no longer on the ship. If nothing else, Cook would eventually look up from her potato collection and realize I wasn't there. A search party would be assembled. I would be rescued, and have a rousing story to tell my new chums at Longshire. In this day and age, I told myself, young nobles do not simply disappear.

Deciding to engage in some vigorous exercise before my inevitable rescue, I began walking down the beach, on the lookout for any dragons or (preferably)

mermaids that might present themselves. The warm sand curved around a small forest, and I decided to follow its course. Probably, the mermaids were feeling shy. I would have to go to them.

Rounding the curve, I saw the shattered hull of The Spotted Narwhale lying on an embankment of rocks, its great mast split in two on the stone. There were several body-shaped lumps laying, unmoving, on the nearby sand.

At this point, (quite reasonably, I think), I began to panic.

I ran, blindly, away from the crashed ship. My feet pounded on the sand as a wail escaped my lips. Rescue wasn't coming. I was stranded. Lost! Doomed—

The sand shifted under my feet, and dropped away. I found myself falling into a dark chasm. My body landed on stone, and I cried out in pain.

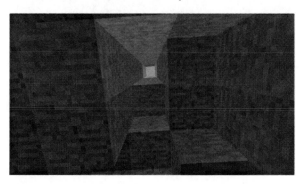

And returning toward me, out of the black, came a long, drawn-out moan. I froze, terrified of the sound. I heard shuffling in the darkness, moving toward me. And, emerging into the light, standing over me, was a body clothed in rags and tatters. As I lay there, frozen with fear, the only thought running through my mind as it leaned toward me was, "This is all Cook's fault."

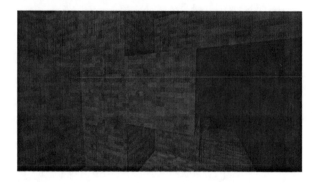

# Chapter 3: The Wizard

Emboldened by fear, I shoved against the decayed creature, breaking its deathgrip on my throat. I scrambled backwards on all fours, trying to put some distance between myself and the walking corpse. It mindlessly pursued me, directly into a beam of sunlight that was still pouring down from the beach above… And the creature burst into flames.

This was less of a relief to me than you might think, because while my subconscious registered a certain happiness at the monster's imminent destruction, in the meantime, I was still at the mercy of a demonic beast with little respect for my personal space. And now, it was on fire.

Leaping to my feet, I circled the chamber, keeping as much distance as possible between myself and the monster. It continued to lunge toward me, even as the flames consumed its body. It cornered me against the cave's cold stone walls, and I thought I had finally met my demise, when the creature abruptly fell over… and disappeared.

Panicked, I flailed my arms, trying to drive away what I was certain was a now-invisible, on-fire dead person. This might seem silly, gentle reader, but please remember that less than an hour ago, I had had no idea a corpse could walk. Once the skeptical mind has overcome the hurdle of undeath, it is remarkably easy to jump to conclusions like "invisible monsters," or "skeletons with arrows," or "little exploding green men." But I get ahead of myself.

After a few short minutes of punching at empty air and quietly screaming to myself, I began to calm down and logically assess the situation, just like I had been trained. I broke it down into the following, easy-to-read format:

1) Monsters were real, death was an illusion, and the facts that I

had until this point believed
supported the universe were lies.

2) I was at the bottom of a hole.

While the first thought probably
deserved more long-term attention, it
was hard to ignore the immediacy of the
second. The sun (apparently my only
protection against assault by any more
violent corpses) would be going down,
soon. Then, I would be trapped, at the
bottom of a hole, in the dark.

I panicked again for a few minutes.

When I checked back in on myself, I
was scratching at the solid stone wall,
desperately trying to climb, but really
only damaging my hands. In frustration
and futility, I welled up my fist and struck
the wall.

And watched, open-mouthed, as the
stone cracked for a moment… and then
healed. Curious, I punched it again,
seeing another crack. Before it could

heal, I punched again, and again. After a few seconds of pugnacious pummeling, a solid cube of stone vanished with a breaking sound. I looked upward at the fading sun, and then redoubled my efforts, punching a staircase into existence.

I emerged from the earth several minutes later, a cubical stairway behind me. The last few feet were the easiest, as the stone (still disappearing in cubic sections) gave way to dirt, which crumbled more quickly under the power of my suddenly mighty fists. I punched through a final layer of dirt, this one covered in grass, and emerged into a sunlit forest clearing. Through the trees, I could see the beach I had awoken on, and the pitiless sea beyond. My protector, the sun, still shown, but was making his (Or her, possibly. I claim no special knowledge of astronomical gender) way across the horizon. I was going to need shelter.

Something strange had happened when I punched the dirt away, that had not occurred while battering the stone: I didn't feel like my hands were going to break with every strike. But also, in place of the broken dirt, I found a small floating brown cube. When I picked it up, it stuck to my hands strangely. I tried to cast it away, and found that I could 'place' it in the world, re-forming the original dirt block. The meaning of this strange phenomenon was obvious, to my hunger-and-thirst-afflicted mind: I had finally become a wizard

I had always suspected, of course. Every young lad, at some time or another, convinces themselves that they are special, chosen, magical. Of course, most of those children are peasants, and wrong. They usually find this out very quickly, when they try to use their magic to… Oh, I don't know. Boil mud? That seems like the sort of thing a peasant would do with magical power

In any case, the un-special peasant child would sit there, with a bucket of raw mud, and be crushed by the knowledge that they were not a wizard. And even I, young noble that I am, had felt the sting of disappointment as my tutors failed to burst into flames when I stared at them and squinted my eyes in a special, wizard-y way. Doubt had crept into my heart. What if.. What if I wasn't a special, magical wizard child?

Now, the truth had become clear, as the harsh sun continued to beat down on my slowly boiling brain: It wasn't that I was an arrogant young idiot with delusions of grandeur. It was that dark wizards had been suppressing my talents since birth, and the shipwreck had knocked them off my trail. Finally, in this wonderful (invisible-monster filled) country, my natural, special snowflake talents could flourish.

I spent several minutes destroying blocks of dirt, and then placing them once again. I reveled in my ability to make the blocks hang off of each other, in all defiance of gravity's vile laws. I stared at some trees and squinted, and tried not to get down when they failed to burst into flame. A lifetime of dark wizard influence can be hard to shake off, I told myself, even for The Chosen Wizard Boy King.

As the sun began to plummet genderlessly into the ocean, I constructed a makeshift shelter out of the damp dirt blocks. So far, my conjuring magic had failed to develop any kind of "bed" or "chair" or "food" spell, but I was not discouraged! Probably I just needed to keep placing and removing dirt blocks, "leveling up" my abilities until all the powers of creations were at hand. Also some food or water or medicine.

In the meantime, I huddled on the stone floor of a small, stinky dirt cave, unable to sleep, and desperately hungry. I listened to the sounds of monstrous moaning, groaning, and screeching as darkness filled the forest. Things moved, unseen, in the black. Glowing eyes, some red, some purple, stared with malice at my tiny shelter. I felt a great, hostile presence, bearing down on me, making it clear that I was unwanted here, that my intrusion would be dealt with swiftly and cruelly. Also, it was cold, and there was nowhere to go to the bathroom.

# Chapter 4: Tool

I was awoken from my miserable semi-slumber by the sound and smell of burning. Looking out of my tiny dirt hovel, I watched as the hordes of monsters that had filled the forest burnt merrily in the morning sunlight. Well, "merrily" was probably a little strong. They burnt, which was enough for me.

During the largely sleepless night, I had developed a plan to enhance my amazing magical powers. Once I was in complete control of my astounding paranormal abilities, I would be able to fly away from this desolate place, and also shoot people who annoyed me with lightning.

But first, I would have to enhance and develop my powers. So far, I knew dirt responded to my talents, and stone did not. But what of wood?! The stuff that trees are made of?!

Apologies, gentle readers. I get excited sometimes, when I've begun untapping the raw powers of creation, and also the only thing I've eaten in several days is lichen growing on a cave floor. I'm sure you understand.

Anyway, I walked over to the nearest tree and began punching it. And, sure enough, my powerful magical fists reduced the mighty oaks or maples or whatever into easily carried blocks. But this time, something strange happened when I held the block in my hand. A sort of grid appeared in my mind. On one side was the wooden block. On the other, a stack of neatly carved planks. Reaching metaphorically forward, I grabbed the planks… And they appeared in my hand.

But not just one plank. Multiple, more than the original block of wood could ever have contained. I had created matter from nothing, violating many of the laws of the universe my tutors had tried to teach me. Clearly, they had been liars, as well as thieves and scoundrels.

I spent the rest of the day honing and experimenting with my skills. I found that I could combine blocks within the grid to create new objects. Several hours were spent, combining everything I could find. Most of my experiments produced nothing, or, useless things, like mud. I suppose, if I was some sort of peasant wizard, I could have boiled the mud, but that wasn't the kind of wizard that I was, was it?

I did make a few things, though. A kind of table that acted as a physical representation of my mental grid, expanding it. A door, which I carefully placed on my dirt cave, and then watched open and close for a few minutes. And a few tools.

I had seen tools before, certainly. Often, when Father's carriage would drive us to see Uncle (Long May He Reign With Sprinkles on Top), we would pass filthy people holding strange objects. When I asked my tutors about them, they had given them bizarre, exotic names. "Axe," was one. "Pickaxe," another. And then, just when I had thought I could perceive the pattern, along came "Shovel," throwing me off. The tutors' explanations of what these 'tools' did were vague by necessity, since no self-respecting teacher would ever use one. Still, going off of memories, shapes, and my incredible intellect, I had created crude facsimiles of the ones I could recall.

I had also used my God-like powers to create a simple wooden sword, in case any more walking corpses decided to get pushy with their opinions about where their hands should go (around my throat, for instance). It wasn't much, but it was more than nothing, and that made it some.

I also… Hm. "Hunted" is probably not the correct word. But I found food, certainly. I stumbled upon it while destroying all of the trees around me with my new "Axe," (crafted from wood, making the whole exercise ghoulishly cannibalistic). In defiance of all proper tree-ly protocol, the destroyed trees left their leaves hanging in the air for several minutes, before they vanished with a pop. Several times, this pop was accompanied with a thump, as a large, juicy apple fell to the ground.

My experience in horticulture is admittedly limited, but even I knew that the trees I was cutting down weren't apple trees. Still, my manners tutor had taught me not to look a gift horse in the mouth, because what if the gift horse has stolen all your apples while you weren't looking? So I took the apples and, famished, ate them.

It was at this point that I began to use my tools in earnest. Using my new wooden "Pickaxe," I cut into the living stone of the earth. This time, instead of simply disappearing, the rock gave up more of the convenient little blocks to me. The pickaxe acted like a kind of "magic-ing wand," enhancing my magical powers and allowing me to overcome more of the dark wizards' (You remember them, they were the ones who had hidden my magical heritage from me, and certainly hadn't been made up during a hunger-fuelled delusion) evil influence.

Then, the wooden "Pickaxe" broke, because I was hitting a piece of rock with a piece of wood, and rock is harder than wood. Which begged the question: Why was I making my tools out of weak, pitiful wood? I threw my broken pickaxe down in disgust, and crafted new tools and weapons from stone. Powerful, invincible stone.

The sun was beginning to set. But this time, I refused to cower in a cave, even if the cave now had a beautifully crafted door. I was a wizard, and I had a sword made of the hardest substance I knew of that wasn't metal or other, harder things. I drew my weapon, and watched the sun fall, ready for whatever came next. It was time to conquer this Isle of Adventure. (If the area was, in fact, an island. I hadn't actually explored that much yet). It was time to prove myself as a warrior, a wizard, and a hero.

# Chapter 5: General Panic

I cried out for my Mother as the scary monsters smacked the remains of my broken weapon from my hands. A spider larger than Father (who was very large) lunged at me, and I turned and ran, tears streaming down my face. An arrow whizzed by my head, fired by a walking skeleton with a permanent, fixed grin. I dodged between the trees, with no idea where my "home" was, and came to face with a calm, smiling green face. Any relief I felt vanished as the placid green figure began to hiss and glow in the sort of way most people don't when trying to be comforting. I leaped away at the last moment, as the creepy creature exploded. On the plus side, the explosion killed the spider, and... disassembled, I guess, would be the appropriate word, the skeleton. On the down side, that still left me, alone, unarmed, in the dark, in a forest full of monsters.

My frantic mind thought back to all of my lessons in tactics, military strategy, and warfare. But as I stumbled through the night, all I could remember was the nasty little song I had written about my military tutor, General Bill "Bloodhawk" Stormheart, notorious for leading several military campaigns that ended in both sides retreating from each other at the same time. Father had hired him to teach me strategy because the General had managed to claim all of these confusing encounters as "Wins," in at least the technical sense, and thus held an undefeated record on the battlefield.

In practice, Stormheart's classes were mostly about picking out the best linens for outfitting a command tent. The general was a great believer in the idea that only comfortable, well-bedded military minds could win battles. Bored, I spent our class time writing mocking songs about him. I include the one that ran through my head that terrible night, hoping the interested reader will find it enjoyable, if not actually singable.

**"The General Bill Stormheart Song"**
(To the tune of Greensleeves)

"Stormheart is dumb,

He stinks of rum,

General-ly awful,

He sucks his thumb."

Ah, young musical genius. In any case, where was I?

Oh, yes. Running through the forest, pursued by a tall, gaunt, purple-eyed creature that screeched horribly every time I looked at it. What a wonderful memory.

Looking around desperately, I searched for high ground, figuring that it would give me better opportunities to defend myself, as well as being ever so slightly closer to the sun, whose light, I figured, was my only chance of survival. Oddly, this DID mimic advice Stormheart had given me, although his reasons for choosing the high ground were mostly linen-related.

The ground curved upward, slowly at first, but increasingly steep. Soon, I found myself leaping from rocky outcropping to rocky outcropping, staying only a few steps ahead of the strange dark figure. Finally, I reached the summit of a large hill, just as a creepy, thin-fingered hand closed around my ankle... And the sun crept over the horizon, spilling its first rays of light.

The creature recoiled as its hand burst into flames, scorching my leg. Kicking feverishly at it, I forced the monster to let go. It fell backwards, plummeting down the slope. Just before it hit the ground, I locked my eyes on its strange purple ones. Letting out one more of its hideous screeches, it vanished. Shaking with fear, I stared at my burnt leg, and then looked out over the landscape around me.

For those of you who have not bothered to look at the title of my little tale, it may come as a great shock to learn that I was, in fact, standing on an island. The sea stretched in every direction, and for a moment, I forgot that I was a Perfect Chosen Wizard Boy, and instead felt very small. I was hurt, alone, and lost. I had never been so far from my home, from Mother, and Father, and Cook, and

Nurse, and all the people who had raised and, perhaps, loved me. I felt utterly alone as I looked over the deserted island, seeing no sign of human habitation except for my cave, and the wrecked ship, and the large castle sitting on the island's far side.

Hm.

# Chapter 6: In Another Castle

Gripping a pale blue sword that sparkled in the fading sunlight, I spun quickly and cut the head off the nearest zombie. I heard the distinctive twang of an arrow firing, and felt something bounce painfully off of my iron armor. Sheathing my sword, Deathbane, I drew my bow, sighted the skeleton in question, and fired. Threat dispatched, I ran across the drawbridge, toward the closed castle gates, as a hissing sound behind me grew stronger. Looking back, I saw the Creeper I had lured here begin to move into the terminal stage of its explosive process. Lunging forward, I grabbed the calmly smiling creature and hurled it with all my might at the gates. The explosion knocked me off my feet, but as the smoke cleared, several cubes had been gouged from the gate's surface, leaving an opening.

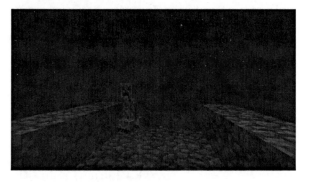

It was weeks later. Weeks of mining, fighting, crafting, and cursing, all leading to this moment. Weeks of realizing that, actually, I was probably not a wizard.

That it was this ISLAND that was magical, and beautiful, and terribly lonely. Weeks, leading to this moment, and the hope of going home.

I had walked up to the gates on that first day, senses ineptly searching for a trap or trick. None had been encountered, only the silence of the forest, and the unyielding gate. A tower loomed over the castle walls. Looking through its wide windows, I saw something shifting and whirling, casting off purple light. It was vaguely familiar, from one of the old storybooks Nurse had read to me when I was younger. It called out to me, and I knew, instinctively: It was a Portal. If I passed through it, it might take me home.

When the gates wouldn't open, even under the most dedicated punching assault, I turned my back on the castle. Returned to the beach, and the home I was slowly building. I constructed great bonfires that burned for hours, trying to draw the attention of passing ships. But none did. Pass, I mean. I mean there were no ships.

In the meantime, I honed my abilities. I descended into the caverns that honeycombed the island, finding valuable ores and experimenting with ways to craft them into useful tools. I hunted the docile creatures that roamed the island during the day, and battled the monsters that overtook it in the night. The only things I stayed away from were the gaunt, tall shadows with the purple eyes. Every time I thought of fighting one, the burn scar on my leg pulsed with pain.

And always, the castle, and the portal, beckoned me. A portal could lead anywhere, but it would certainly lead somewhere. The island was beautiful, but it was dangerous, and I had a home to return to, somewhere. I had a Father to speak to, a Mother to hug. I vowed that I would not die without seeing them again.

Delving deep, I found diamonds, gleaming above churning lava. I constructed my blade, Deathbane, and crafted a suit of armor from the iron I found in abundance down there. And then, setting my heart on the portal as my only way to return home, I devised my plan, reckless, dangerous, and ultimately effective, to breach the castle gates.

The castle courtyard was swarming with zombies, skeletons, and giant spiders. They moved in a creepy unison, rarely getting in each other's way as they poured from the hole in the wall. I laughed as I entered battle with them, Deathbane cutting as fast as my arm could move. I took hits, certainly, but the armor took the brunt of the blows. I pushed through the horde, and ran for the tower that dominated the courtyard's center.

Throwing the door open, pursued by the slow-moving undead, I practically flew up the stairs. Legs that once complained at being asked to walk to the pantry and kick a servant had been hardened by weeks of hard work and exercise. Finally, I reached the door at the top of the spire. Steeling myself for a moment, I threw it open, and looked upon a scene from my own nightmares.

There were five of them, the shadows, waiting for me in the room that housed the portal. I locked eyes with one, and, screeching in their terrible way, it vanished for a moment, then appeared directly in front of me, striking with its shapeless arms. Acting on instinct, I stabbed forward with Deathbane, skewering the creature. There was a smell of sulfur, and the creature vanished, leaving only a strange, cat-eyed jewel glimmering on the floor. Three of the others surrounded me, striking viciously and disappearing when I tried to counter.

Slowly, I wore through their defenses, dispatching the monsters as my strength slowly waned. Soon, they were dead (or gone, at least, since nothing on this island ever seemed to leave a corpse), and I was bloodied and weary. There was only one of the creatures left, still standing, unmoving, where it had been when I entered the room. I ran toward it, eyes locked, wondering if it was the same shadow that had given me my scar. And just as I struck, it vanished… and, off-balance, I fell into the portal.

The world began to shimmer and change. I felt like my body was being pulled in a thousand directions. As I looked back at the world I was leaving, I saw the shadow, the slender man, look at me.

Its expressionless face seemed to smile. It was a smile from a child's darkest dream. I screamed… And vanished.

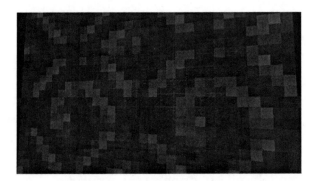

# Epilogue: Somewhere in the Universe

If you are reading this, Gentle Reader, then presumably you have found the portal. It will not transport me back to the island, but apparently non-living things can move back through it. I leave this record as a guide to the ways of living and thriving on my Isle of Adventure. Once you know its tricks, survival there is not hard. It is a good place, I realize, now. Better than some, in any case.

The portal does not lead home. At least, not to mine, and, I pray, not to yours. If you are considering the proposition, I must repeat, and loudly. DO NOT USE THE PORTAL. I will not describe what it is like here. But I find myself nostalgic for the Isle, and its comforts. And even its creatures.

I have not given up on trying to make my way home. A vow made is not forsaken lightly. There is more exploring to do, more discovery. But I am not optimistic, gentle reader. There is little room for optimism in this place. Or humor. Or silliness.

Once, I was a noble, son of a King's younger brother (May he be happy, and treat Mother well). Once, I was spoiled, and frivolous, the kind of foolish boy who would blame a Cook for his own dark fate. Once, I had a name. But the world changes, and many frivolous things burn away, given sufficient heat and time.

And so, with regards, gentle reader, I bid you farewell, and sign this journal, this missive of my time on the Isle of Adventure, only as

-X

PS: If you find my cave, dig beneath the block of blue wool in the corner. Take what you find there, with my blessing. The diamond pickaxe served me well, and the map is as accurate as I can make it. As to the recipe for stewed apples, I make no promises. I have omitted sugar from it.

I found it to be too sweet.

CPSIA information can be obtained at www.ICGtesting.com
Printed in the USA
LVOW07s1010230815

451201LV00016B/476/P

9 781494 985110